Fergus's
Upside-down Day

First published in 1994 in Great Britain by
Piccadilly Press Ltd, London
www.piccadillypress.co.uk

Text and illustrations copyright © Tony Maddox 1994

This 2010 edition published by Sandy Creek by arrangement with Piccadilly Press

Sandy Creek
122 Fifth Avenue
New York, NY 10011

ISBN: 978 1 4351 2333 5

1 3 5 7 9 10 8 6 4 2

Printed and bound in China

Fergus's
Upside-down Day

Tony Maddox

Sandy Creek

"We're off to market, Fergus!"
called Farmer Bob.
"Look after the animals and make sure
they don't get into any trouble."

"A nice quiet day!" thought Fergus.
"Nothing to do but sleep in the sun."
He looked around. The hens were in
the yard, the ducks were by the pool
and the pigs were in their pen.

In the orchard, the goat was looking
for fallen apples and the cow was grazing
in the meadow.

All seemed well.
"I think I'll bury my bone behind
the barn," thought Fergus.

But when he returned sometime later,
there was no sign of the hens, or the ducks,
or the pigs, or the goat, or the cow!

Then he noticed the open farmhouse door!
He looked inside to see the hens
and the ducks . . . watching television!

He went through to the kitchen.
There were the pigs . . . eating spaghetti
and baked beans!

He rushed upstairs to the bedroom to find the goat . . . wearing the new hat and coat that Farmer Bob's wife had just bought!

BATHROOM

And when he opened the bathroom door,
he couldn't believe his eyes . . .

. . . the cow was taking a bubble bath!

Suddenly the clock struck four! Farmer Bob
and his wife would be back any minute!
"Woof, Woof, Woof!" went Fergus
as he hurried the animals outside.

Quickly, he switched off the television, washed the plates and had just finished tidying up when Farmer Bob's truck pulled into the yard.

"Phew! Just in time!" thought Fergus.
But had he forgotten anything? He tried
hard to remember. What about the cow . . .
. . . was she still in the bath?
Fergus groaned and closed his eyes.

The next thing he heard was
Farmer Bob's voice.
"Wake up Fergus. We're home!
Bet you've had a nice quiet day!"
"Humph!" thought Fergus.
"A quiet day! It's been an
upside-down day!"

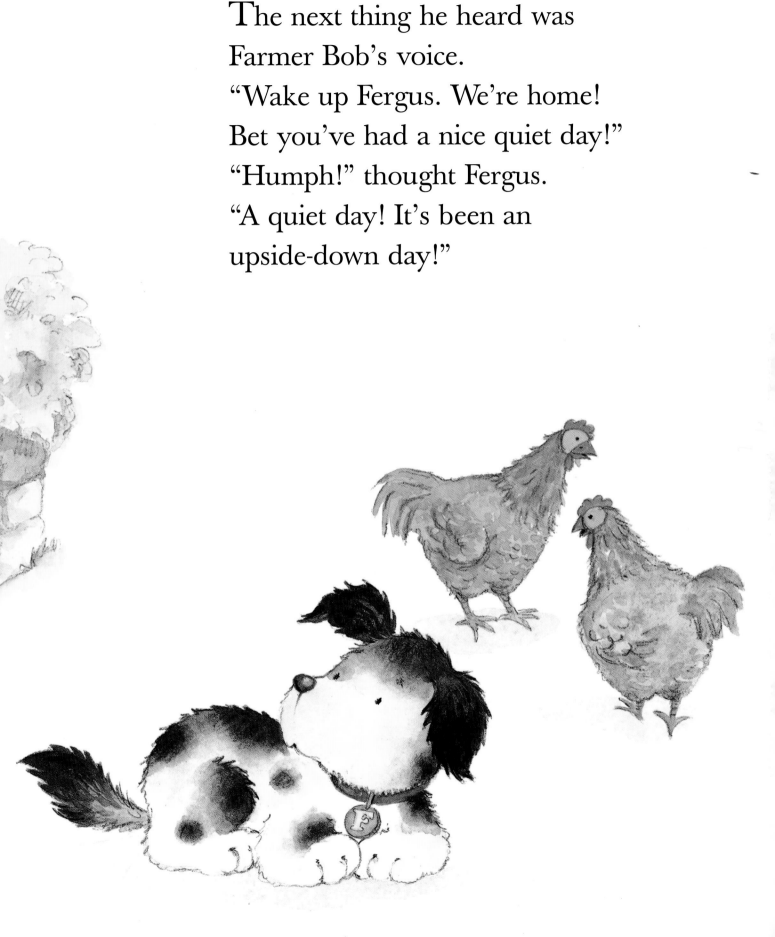

But when he looked around the farm, everything seemed quite normal, and much to his surprise, the cow was back in the meadow.

Fergus gave a big sigh of relief.
"It must have been a dream after all!"
he thought.

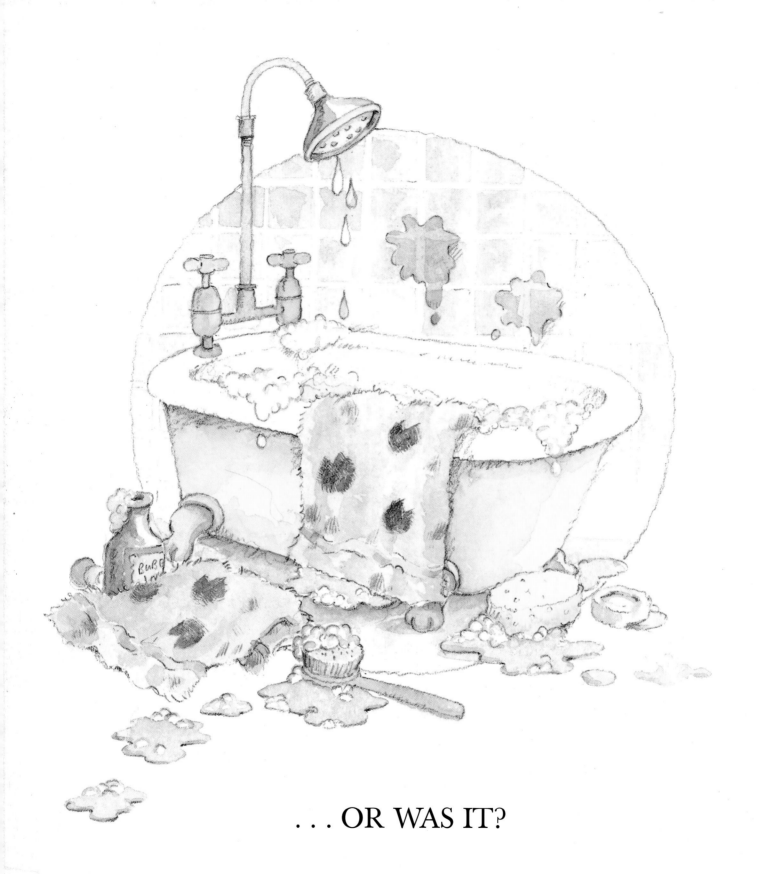

. . . OR WAS IT?